JUV
F
EME

JO'S TROUBLED HEART

THE LITTLE WOMEN JOURNALS™
by *Charlotte Emerson*
from *Avon Books*

AMY'S TRUE PRIZE
BETH'S SNOW DANCER
JO'S TROUBLED HEART
MEG'S DEAREST WISH

Madame Alexander®
ALEXANDER DOLL COMPANY, INC.

The Little Women Journals™

— JO'S TROUBLED HEART —

Charlotte Emerson

Illustrations by Kevin Wasden

AVON BOOKS NEW YORK

AVON BOOKS
A division of
The Hearst Corporation
1350 Avenue of the Americas
New York, New York 10019

Library of Congress Cataloging in Publication Data:

Emerson, Charlotte.
    Jo's troubled heart / Charlotte Emerson.—1st ed.
        p.   cm.—(Little women journals)
Summary: As Christmas approaches, Jo March finds herself unable to control her quick
temper even though it causes strife in the family and threatens the publication of her first
story in the newspaper.
[1. Behavior—Fiction.   2. Sisters—Fiction.   3. Christmas—Fiction.   4. Family life—New
England—Fiction.   5. New England—Fiction.]   I. Alcott, Louisa May, 1832–1888. Little
women.   II. Title.   III. Series: Emerson, Charlotte. Little women journals.
PZ7.E5835Jo   1997   97-7280
[Fic]—dc21   CIP

First Avon Books Printing: February 1998

TABLE OF CONTENTS

Contents

JO'S TROUBLED HEART

CHAPTER ONE

Bah, Humbug!

"*W*hy does November always seem longer than any other month?" Meg March asked, staring out through a windowpane streaked with rain.

"I'm positive it has at *least* forty-five days in it," her sister Amy said with a sigh.

Beth spread the tea cloth over the table and smoothed it. "The month is almost over. And then comes December. And December means—"

"Christmas!" the three girls chorused.

With a happy smile, Meg turned from the window and joined Amy and Beth by the fire. "I don't expect much this year with Father away," Meg said. Their father was serving as a chaplain to Union soldiers in Washington, D.C. "But Marmee did promise me a new sash for my tarlatan dress."

"What I really want is an easel, just like a real artist," Amy said dreamily. "And pencils, and a new blue ribbon, and a cameo to put on a black velvet ribbon around my neck—"

"Is that all?" Meg teased.

Amy shook her golden curls. "And an orange."

Beth and Meg laughed at such a humble end to a grand beginning.

Beth looked toward the door anxiously. "Where's Jo? She should have been home by now. The weather is so fierce."

"She's probably tramping through puddles," Meg said with a sigh. At sixteen, she was the oldest of the girls and took her position seriously. "Our Jo loves a good storm."

"But the tea is getting cold," Amy said wistfully. "And Hannah made her special ginger cake today. She said a body needs cheering in bad weather. I must say, this rain is positively *matricious*." At eleven, Amy struggled to perfect a more adult vocabulary.

"You mean *malicious*, dear, I think," Meg said,

affectionately tugging on Amy's curls. "And weather can't be malicious, though people can," she added.

"Well, that ginger cake looks *delicious*," Amy said longingly.

"Who said rain can't be malicious?" Jo bellowed from the hall where she was shaking out her umbrella. "This rain is designed to torment Jo March personally. I'm certain that the wind was laughing when it turned my umbrella inside out."

Jo strode briskly into the room, shaking raindrops from her thick chestnut hair. She was tall for fifteen, and her long legs and arms had a habit of accidentally knocking over sugar bowls, creamers, and teacups. "If only you didn't *gesture* so much," Meg often complained.

Now Jo shook out her wet skirts, sending raindrops flying. She sprayed the cat, who gave a loud *meow* and quickly jumped up on a table, almost upsetting a lamp.

Meg frowned, but Beth jumped up and ran toward her. "You're soaked through, Jo! Come sit by the fire."

Jo smiled as Beth tugged her to an armchair close to the fire. Beth was only thirteen, but she took care of them all. Meg ran for a towel to dry

Jo's hair. Amy, using her best formal manner, poured Jo a cup of steaming tea and added plenty of sugar.

Jo unlaced her wet boots and placed them on the hearth to dry. "Well, now, this *is* jolly," she said, pouring the hot tea into her saucer and blowing on it. "All I've heard today is cross words. And my name being called—'Josey-phine! Josey-phine!'—all the livelong day."

"Aunt March is no better?" Beth asked anxiously.

Shaking her head, Jo tilted the saucer and drank. Meg lifted an eyebrow disapprovingly.

"Oh, hang manners, Meg, the tea is too hot to drink and I'm so cold," Jo said cheerfully. "Yes, my Bethy, Aunt March is no better. She's a good soul, and I know she feels miserable with a bad cold, but must she make the entire household miserable along with her?"

"I'm sure you worked very hard," Beth said, rubbing Jo's stockinged feet.

"All I want from life is one tiny, thrilling adventure," Jo continued, enjoying the luxury of complaining about her day to her family while the cold rain beat against the windowpanes. "And all I get are tiresome complaints and running endlessly for handkerchiefs and cups of beef tea."

"Poor Aunt March," Beth said. "It's so dreadful to be ill."

"Poor Jo March, who has to nurse her," Jo said with a grin. "Bless her cranky good soul, I cannot please her these days. Either my voice is too harsh when I read to her—no matter how softly I speak— or I haven't fixed her shawl well enough around her shoulders, or my hand isn't steady enough when I spoon the broth into her mouth, or her pillows aren't arranged correctly—"

Jo made a sweeping gesture to demonstrate her pillow-arranging. Unfortunately, her teacup was balanced rather unsteadily on her knee. The cup went flying, along with the warm, sweet liquid. A brown stain appeared on her pretty gingham dress.

"Christopher Columbus!" Jo exclaimed, jumping up. She rubbed at the stain with her handkerchief. The stain spread, and a soiled handkerchief now added to the disaster.

"Jo, wait!" Beth cried.

"You're making it worse!" Meg scolded, while she dabbed carefully at the stain with a napkin.

Jo collapsed into the armchair. "And it's my best everyday dress, too. Aren't we supposed to pay a call on those terribly fashionable Moffat girls?"

Meg sighed. "This week, I'm afraid. Oh, Jo."

"And I can't wear my good gown, because that one has an ink stain near the hem," Jo said worriedly.

"Really, Jo," Meg scolded her. "Whatever made you wear your silk gown while you were writing?"

"It's my favorite dress!" Jo exclaimed. "Burgundy is such a *masterful* color. I thought it would inspire me. I didn't notice that my pen was dripping until it was too late."

"So swept up in your own tales," Beth said with a sigh. "That's our Jo."

"Your foolish Jo," Jo said. "Now I've ruined my gown."

"All is not lost, Jo," Meg said, her pretty face shining. "I have a surprise for you!" She hurried out of the room.

Jo poured herself another cup of tea, and Amy cut her a slice of Hannah's ginger cake. When Meg returned, she was holding Jo's best dress in her arms.

"You'll never see the stain now," Meg said, holding up the dress for Jo to admire. A deep flounce now adorned the hem.

"Oh, Meg," Jo said, knitting her brow. "You know I'm not one for fine trimmings. You're such a good sister to sew for me, but must you ruffle me up? It shall be the death of me."

"What's wrong with the ruffle?" Amy asked, rising to Meg's defense as usual. "It's pretty."

"It's so . . . big," Jo said.

"So was the ink stain," Meg pointed out, hurt.

But Jo didn't notice Meg's downcast look. "If there is one thing I can't abide, it's a big, fluttery ruffle," she declared. "It makes me look like a silly goose, trying to be girlish when I'm not in the least." She put down her teacup with a clatter. "Why can't I dress like a boy and be done with it!"

"Because you *are* a girl," Meg said, her exasperated tone covering up her hurt feelings. She folded up the dress in a quick gesture and placed it on a chair.

"Yes, I'm a girl," said Jo with a dramatic sigh. "And I want to be a hero. I want to climb mountains, or even have a tutor at home like Teddy so that I can go off to college one day."

"Teddy" was Jo's pet name for Theodore Laurence, whom the rest of the sisters called "Laurie." He lived in the grand estate next door with his grandfather. He was more than a good neighbor to the girls. He was the dear brother they never had, the friend they always wanted, and an enthusiastic partner in any scheme they proposed.

"In order to study with a tutor and go to college,

you'd need riches, as Laurie has," Meg pointed out, "as well as trousers."

"Quite right, Meg," Jo said good-naturedly. "So I shall have to content myself with reading to an old woman and making good strong pots of tea." She stuck her feet out to catch the warmth of the flames, wiggling her stockinged toes. "I think I have it the hardest of all of you."

"Do you?" Meg asked with a superior look.

"I do," Jo said decidedly. "Why Meg, you just have to straighten pinafores and teach the King girls how to keep Paris and Tangiers straight in geography lessons. Beth, bless your heart, you do so much, but dusting and keeping house leaves plenty of time for reading and dreaming. And Amy is luckiest of all. She gets to go to school all day!"

"That's the silliest thing I ever heard," Meg said, sitting down primly. She frowned at Jo. "It isn't easy being a governess. I have my hands full with the King girls. Every day, there are all sorts of problems that pop up and tempers to be tamed."

"And going to school is dreadful," Amy said. "Especially when everyone laughs at your bonnets and notices the holes in your gloves."

Beth didn't say a word in her own defense. She

ducked her head and pushed Marmee's slippers closer to the fire to warm them.

"Marmee would be disappointed to hear you talk so, Jo," Meg told her sister sharply. "Each of us should find pleasure in our duties, not look at them as burdens."

Jo felt Beth's small hand slip into hers. Beth knew that Jo's grumbling was seldom serious. She knew how a long walk through cold rain could make a body feel rather grumpy. Jo softly stroked Beth's shiny hair.

"Besides," Amy said, "Christmas is coming, and Christmas is always wonderful."

Jo couldn't help grinning. It was hard not to smile at little Amy, who started dreaming about presents months before Christmas.

Jo ducked her head and poked the fire, mischievously hiding her smile from her sisters.

"Bah, humbug!" she growled. "What no one cares to admit is that Ebenezer Scrooge is right. Christmas is merely an excuse for perfectly serious people to act silly."

Meg arched an eyebrow. "Since when do you object to silliness?"

Jo stood up and struck a pose, using the poker as a walking stick. "If Mr. Dickens will pardon me,

I'll write a more fitting ending for his tale," she said in a deep, gruff voice. "The ghosts fail to convince Scrooge that Christmas should be honored in his heart. Bob Crachit agrees, and they petition the Queen to rewrite the calendar. From now on, December the twenty-fourth shall be followed by December the twenty-sixth. No presents will be given, and turkeys and geese shall be spared throughout the land!"

"Here, here! I like that part," Beth cheered.

"Tiny Tim signs on as an apprentice in Scrooge's firm," Jo continued in a ringing tone. "And Bob Crachit is made partner. They celebrate their victory by eating porridge for dinner and doing nothing special at all!"

Meg, Beth, and Amy burst out laughing. Even Jo finally gave in and had to laugh at her own nonsense. And when Marmee entered, her tiredness was forgotten as she beamed at happy faces warmed by firelight.

CHAPTER TWO

Inspiration at Midnight

$\mathcal{T}$hat night, near midnight, Jo woke out of a dream with a start. The moon had risen high in the sky. Now it painted a silvery path across her coverlet. Jo would have liked to admire it, but if she stayed in bed, she would fall back asleep.

She swung her legs over the bed. Yawning, she tugged her warm nightcap down on her forehead. Then she drew a thick shawl around her ivory nightgown and put on her slippers. Glancing out the window, she noticed that the cold rain had turned to snow. No wonder she felt so cold!

She opened the lid of her trunk and slipped out a bundle. Then she headed out of her room.

In the hall, she paused to listen to the quiet breathing of her sisters. All of Orchard House was asleep. Jo tiptoed past Marmee's door and climbed up the garret stairs.

The air was bitter cold up in the attic, but Jo had piled plenty of quilts on the old sofa, and she quickly snuggled underneath them. Reaching over to the desk, she took up her pen.

Lately she'd been so busy during the day that her writing time had shrunk to nothing. She hadn't even had a chance to write in her journal. Aunt March needed her every minute. And with Christmas coming, the girls' workbaskets were full. There were socks and mittens to knit for the soldiers. The upcoming winter would be a harsh one without warm things.

Jo let out a guilty sigh. She often wrote in the attic at night, for privacy. But she knew that Marmee would not approve of her leaving her warm bed so late at night and working into the early hours.

Still, sleep was out of the question when a story was burning in her, begging to be written. And if the story turned out to be as good as she thought it would, she would reap grand rewards.

With a longing glance at her half-finished manuscript, Jo drew her journal toward her. She needed to pen a few lines before she got down to hard work.

It is so dreadfully hard to leave my warm bed at night. But I feel sure that this story deserves my hard work. The Patriot Gazette has a large circulation, and it pays the most for stories. I fear my old yarns are not professional enough. This one shall be!

Best of all, I'm putting in every element my sisters adore. I've given the hero and heroine our very favorite names, Delano and Angelica. There is an evil count with a mustache, just to give Beth delicious chills. There is a fainting scene—how Amy shall love to practice her fainting skills! There are betrayals and reversals, to keep Meg guessing. There's a dungeon, a drowning, and a suicide. It's a grisly, thrilling, romantic tale, just as we all crave!

But it isn't only the story that shall be my gift to my sisters. I shall spend all the money I earn on wonderful presents for Christmas. Imagine how happy Meg shall be when she finds a new satin sash under the tree! And Amy shall have her easel, and Marmee *a thick warm scarf, and Beth . . . well, I haven't quite decided what I shall buy for Beth. But I shall find something wonderful for my girl. Perhaps a pretty white cage for her canary, or a portfolio for her music.*

Jo smiled, thinking of Christmas morning. Then she shook her head and bent down to write again.

But I shan't have anything to give if I sit daydreaming. And now to work.

Jo closed her journal and pulled the manuscript pages toward her. She leafed through them, nodding at the story's complicated twists and turns. Instead of one villain, there are three, and they are brothers. They live in a crumbling Italian castle that overlooks the crashing sea. Together they plot against a dashing stepbrother, who is the hero Delano, of course.

Handsome Delano arrives at the castle to claim his part of the family fortune. But the brothers plot and scheme against him. They even try to foil his romance with the plucky and beautiful Angelica.

Jo frowned. The only trouble was, something in the story wasn't quite working. Something was missing. The tale felt to Jo like an arrow that *almost* hit the target.

It didn't feel *real* somehow. But she felt confident that the more she worked on it, the better it would be. It was certainly worth losing a few hours of sleep to fix it.

Of course, during the day she paid the price for her late nights. Often she found her eyelids drooping. Sometimes her temper was short. But she was certain she could finish the story in a week or so. All she had to do was keep waking herself at midnight.

Jo blew on her cold fingers to warm them. "Artists must suffer, Jo March, so why should you be any different?" she muttered. "Think of how happy Christmas morning will be for your sisters!"

She wrapped her cold fingers around her pen and began to write.

Delano froze against the cold castle wall. The figure in the dripping garments came toward him, and a hand like an eagle's claw closed upon his wrist!

"Jo! Jo! Wake up, dear. It's past time for you to be up and about."

Meg's sweet voice drifted into Jo's dreams. She burrowed deeper into her pillow.

"Jo!"

Now she felt a gentle shake. "I've called you three times now. You *must* get up."

Longing to slide back into her dreams, Jo dragged her eyes open. The sun streamed through the curtains of her bedroom. Meg's long braid hung over one shoulder. She had one boot off and one boot on. Obviously, she had interrupted her dressing to make sure Jo was up.

"It *can't* be morning," Jo groaned.

Meg opened the curtains wider. "Either that, or the moon is remarkably bright. Look at the beautiful snow!"

Marmee paused in the doorway. "Hurry, girls. Hannah has breakfast on the table."

"Coming, Marmee," Jo called, sitting up.

"I've laid out your dress and apron," Meg said as she hurried to the door, her skirts swishing. "Hurry!"

"Hurry, hurry, hurry," Jo grumbled. "Why is it that I always *do* hurry, and I'm always behind?"

But Meg's tone and Marmee's warning made her spring out of bed. She managed to get herself dressed and her hair bundled into a net in record time. She charged downstairs and skidded down the hall to the dining room.

The rest of the family was halfway through their breakfast as Jo slid into her place. Only the lift of an eyebrow told her that Marmee didn't approve of her tardiness.

"I'm sorry, Marmee," Jo said meekly as she poured milk in her tea.

"This is the third morning this week that you've overslept, Jo," Marmee said. "Are you sure you're feeling well?"

Jo swallowed a mouthful of toast. "Quite well. I'm just a bit tired." She tried to suppress a yawn. She knew Meg would give her a disapproving look. But once the urge to yawn begins, it is almost impossible to stop it.

"It looks as though you're more than a bit tired," Marmee observed with a gentle frown.

Amy began to chatter about the day ahead, but Jo was too tired to listen. She drank her tea quickly and poured another cup, but it failed to give her energy. Her head drooped, and she dropped her knife on her plate with a clatter.

Marmee rose. "Jo!" She bent over to press her cheek against Jo's forehead. Jo leaned against Marmee's softness like she would against a warm pillow.

"No fever," Marmee murmured.

Beth looked at Jo, concerned. "Maybe you're getting Aunt March's cold."

"I never get colds," Jo said, snuggling against

18

Marmee sleepily. Marmee stroked her hair, and Jo sighed in contentment.

"No dear, you just get a red nose, and a clogged head, and you sneeze dreadfully loud and shout, 'Well, God bless me!'" Marmee teased gently.

Jo laughed, still resting against Marmee. "Oh, is that what you mean by a cold?"

"Why don't I take Aunt March some of Hannah's broth this morning?" Beth suggested quietly. "I don't mind, truly." Jo shot her a questioning look. Beth was shy, and Aunt March's harshness sometimes frightened her. "That way you can stay at home today," she added.

"Beth, you're an angel, but I know very well that Aunt March is your dragon," Jo said, straightening up. "I can't let you."

"I think it's a capital idea," Meg said. "Jo, you haven't been yourself lately. A day at home is just what you need."

"I agree," Marmee said. She smiled at Beth. "Thank you, dearie."

"Well, Aunt March is feeling too poorly to bark at you much," Jo mused. "And I suppose your quiet ways would suit her today. I'll take care of your housework, Bethy."

19

Jo felt better already at the prospect of a quiet day. Now she would have time to finish her story!

"I approve of life when it turns around and surprises you," Jo announced, reaching for another piece of toast. Just knowing that she would not have to answer to Aunt March's cross moods that morning made her feel more awake. "I'm ready for a different sort of day."

CHAPTER THREE

Topsy-Turvy

$\mathcal{T}$he usual bustle of departure did not include Jo that morning. She helped Beth on with her cloak and bonnet. She placed hot turnovers in Meg and Beth's hands, for warmth and nutrition. She found Amy's slate and her left glove. She stood next to Marmee at the window and waved goodbye until the girls were out of sight.

Marmee left a few minutes later, her basket full of Hannah's freshly baked bread. She was taking it to the church, where the ladies were gathering to work on holiday baskets.

Jo surveyed the table. The jumble of breakfast things reminded her that she had work to do.

"First, the washing up," she told herself. "Then, a little dusting and cleaning. With my energy, I'm sure I can get the chores done in half the time that Beth takes. And then . . . Oh, bliss! Writing in front of a blazing fire."

She tied her apron more tightly around her waist and set to work.

Impatient Jo was not content to bring the dishes to the kitchen a few at a time. She stacked as many as she could, and hooked teacups onto her fingers. Opening the kitchen door with her hip, she started for the sink. A teacup rattled on a saucer, then toppled over.

Jo gasped and held the dishes closer as Hannah reached out and caught the cup in the nick of time.

"Sakes, Miss Jo, be careful!" Hannah scolded. "I'm boiling up the jam today, so mind that pot. And are you trying to break every piece of china your blessed mother owns?"

"I'm just trying to be efficient, Hannah," Jo told her.

"Efficiency doesn't mean breaking teacups, if you don't mind my saying so," Hannah told her. "And you can't wash dishes with cold water. Best put a pot to boil on the fire."

"Oh, I forgot," Jo said as she ran for the broom. "I'll do that now."

By the time she'd finished the washing up, Jo longed for a nap. But there was still dusting and cleaning to be done. When she returned to the parlor, the fire had gone out.

"Tarnation!" Jo exclaimed. The room was cold and dark, and a gust of wind had sent ashes onto the carpet.

Then she discovered that the woodpile was low. She'd have to chop more kindling. That had been her chore the past Saturday, and she had neglected it.

"And Beth didn't say a word, the dear," Jo said, tying on her scarf. "She was planning to chop it herself, I suppose."

Mindful of her near miss in the kitchen, Jo didn't hurry as she chopped the wood into kindling.

"For I don't mind smashing a cup, but an ankle is another matter," she told herself cheerfully.

She built another fire, rocking back on her heels to admire the roaring blaze.

"There. That should keep me warm while I do the dusting," she murmured.

At least dusting was easy. She flew about the room with the rag, attacking chair arms and vases, books and ledges, doorknobs and tables. When she swiped at a bookcase and her dustcloth slipped behind it, Jo stamped her foot with irritation. There was no time to dig through the pantry for another clean cloth.

Thinking fast, she bunched up her apron and used it to swipe along the surfaces. A stroke of genius! she thought, congratulating herself.

The morning was barreling on, and she still had chores to finish!

When she reached the small table near Marmee's chair, she hurriedly ran her apron along the edge and turned toward the mantle. Then, behind her, she heard a crash.

"Oh, dear!" Jo turned and saw that in her haste, she had knocked Marmee's precious china figurine off the table. It lay broken on the hearth.

"Not again! Hannah will scold me so! And Marmee will be heartbroken. Oh, I am a fright!"

Jo picked up the pieces and placed them carefully in her apron. The delicate china shepherdess was now headless.

She sighed. "How could I have been so careless!"

"Maybe from running around like a tornado instead of using a careful touch," Hannah said, bustling into the room in her head scarf and long coat. "I peeked in here earlier and saw you buzzing around like a bee."

"You're right, Hannah," Jo said ruefully. "I was trying to get the chore done in half the time."

"Chores take their own time," Hannah said kindly. "Now, don't fret, Miss Jo. Look, it's a good break. The little head snapped off clean."

"Like she'd gone to her dismal death by guillotine in the French revolution," Jo said with a shiver, enjoying the ghoulish thought.

"Save the stories for your books, Miss Jo," Hannah said, laughing. "What you need is glue, not imagination. And there's some in the cupboard. Set to work and make it right. You know Miz March won't blame you."

"Of course she won't, she's such a dear," Jo said. "Thank you, Hannah."

Jo started off to look for the glue.

"Mind my jam while I'm gone, will you, Miss Jo?" Hannah called, heading for the front door. "I've already added the sugar. You'll just have to stir it every so often so it won't stick. I've got to go to the market, then bring this basket to the Hummels."

"I'll watch the jam," Jo promised distractedly as

she tried to fit the head of the shepherdess back on the body.

"Best put some newspapers down for that chore," was Hannah's last bit of advice before hurrying out the door, basket on her arm.

But by the time Jo stirred the jam and fetched the glue, she'd forgotten the advice. Then she remembered in the middle of her chore and ran for the papers. In placing them on the table, she upset the glue pot.

"Oh, the confounded thing!"

Jo ran for the dust rag to soak up the glue. A moment later she stopped in her tracks, remembering that she'd dropped it behind the bookcase. She would have to use her apron once again.

Repairing the figurine was a messy business. Her fingers got stuck on the paper, and she had to run to wash them before the glue dried. She wished for Amy's delicate fingers, or Meg's careful ones, as she placed the head back on the shepherdess. Now the figure looked cockeyed.

"It will have to do, that's all." Jo set the figure on the windowsill to dry.

When she tried to clean up the newspapers, she realized that they'd stuck to the table.

"Tarnation!" Jo thundered. She was glad Meg

and Marmee were not about. She'd done nothing but use slang and lose her temper this morning!

Using hot water and a rag, Jo got as much of the paper up as she could. Then she remembered Hannah's instructions. . . .

"The jam!".

Back in the kitchen, a mess of bubbling jam met her horrified eyes. The boiling pots had overflowed onto the stove.

"What a confoundedly *sticky* morning," Jo exclaimed, setting to with a wet rag.

Her apron was streaked with dust and dirt from being used as a dustrag. Glue had made flecks of newspaper adhere to the cloth. There was still newspaper stuck to the dining table. Glue was on the carpet, and now jam was all over the stove. It had been a disaster of a morning.

"Nothing done that can't be undone," Jo said aloud, trying to cheer herself.

Then she heard the sound of the door and running footsteps.

"Jo?"

It was Meg. Wiping her hands on her soiled apron, Jo hurried into the parlor. With Meg were her two charges, Lucy and Bettina King. They stared at Jo curiously with eyes as dark and shiny as buttons.

Meg drew her aside. "Jo, you must do me a favor," she said breathlessly. "I know this was to be a morning of relaxation for you. But can you watch my charges for me? They won't be a bit of trouble, I promise you."

CHAPTER FOUR

Pinafores and Predicaments

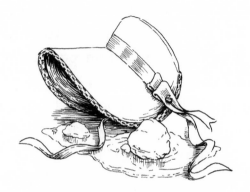

*T*he two young King girls peered at Jo.

"What a funny girl," Bettina said.

"What's stuck to her head?" Lucy asked.

Jo reached up. A scrap of newspaper had stuck to her untidy locks. She tore it out, bringing a good number of hairs along with it.

"Ouch!" she exclaimed. She made a comical face, but the girls didn't laugh.

"Why did you do *that?*" Bettina asked scornfully.

Lucy examined her with sharp dark eyes. "Your apron is *very* dirty," she observed.

Bettina stuck her tongue out at her. Jo had to pinch herself to restrain her impulse to return the gesture.

Jo turned to Meg. In a low voice, she asked, "Do explain to me, Meg, why I must watch them?"

Meg had missed Bettina's naughty gesture. "I'm sorry, Jo, but there's nothing else to be done. You see, Mrs. King had planned an outing for the girls to visit their cousins."

Meg leaned closer. "Though actually," she whispered, "I suspect she just wanted them out of the way, for she's giving a grand ball this evening. At any rate, when we arrived at the Van Semples, I found the household in an uproar. The children *and* their mother have influenza. The cook had gone to town, and the housekeeper was burning with fever and unable to tend to anyone. I must fetch the doctor."

Meg's eyes were anxious, and Jo impulsively gave her a hug. "Of course I'll watch the girls for you," she said warmly. "Don't worry about a thing, Meg."

Jo peeked over Meg's shoulder at the girls. They had removed their coats, and now sat primly in their starched white pinafores. It seemed unnatural to Jo that two young girls could sit so still and not giggle or explore.

"But whatever shall I *do* with them?" Jo whispered.

"Amuse them. You're so good with young children," Meg said, hurriedly pulling on her gloves. Before Jo could say another word, her sister was sweeping out the door.

Jo turned to face her charges.

Bettina nudged her sister and pointed to a worn place in the carpet. She made a face.

The trouble is, Jo thought to herself, these two don't seem to be children at all.

By the time an hour had passed, Jo had to admit that she'd met her match in six-year-old Lucy and eight-year-old Bettina. The King girls were like no children she'd ever met. They didn't laugh at silly things or silly faces. They had no interest in Beth's dolls or the canary. They didn't want to take a good tramp in the garden because there was snow on the ground! They greeted the idea of putting on their very own play with a large yawn.

After Jo read to them from her favorite old fairy tale book, Bettina only sniffed and said, "Fairy stories are silly."

"They aren't *real*," Lucy said scornfully.

Jo stared helplessly at her two young charges. How did Meg cope with two girls with absolutely no imaginations?

"Please amuse yourselves for a few minutes," Jo said grimly. She put the book aside. "I must tend to the jam."

"It should be done by now," Bettina said. "You've kept running to the kitchen."

"Miss March doesn't fly about so," Lucy said. "Why do you scurry about like a wild goose? And don't you have servants to make jam?"

"We do our own chores in this household," Jo said, holding on to her sweetness with a forced smile.

"How dreadful for you," Lucy said.

"Lucy, Mother says we should be *kind* to inferiors," Bettina whispered to her sister, loud enough for Joe to hear.

Inferiors! Jo wanted to launch into a scathing lecture, but thought better of it. Quickly she gathered her skirts and rushed from the room. Angelic little Bettina, with her ruffles and ribbons and superior attitude, would have to wait.

The jam had cooled and thickened, and Jo spooned it into the jam pots. At least she could manage this task without creating a disaster. She wiped up the counter and decided to label the jars later. She was only halfway done, but she didn't want to leave the girls alone too long.

When she rushed out of the kitchen, she saw that the girls were now at the long dining table. They were quiet, patiently amusing themselves with some private game. Jo stopped, relieved. Perhaps, if they amused themselves, she could sit at the table with them and work on her story.

"Sticky," Bettina said.

"Here, glue this one," Lucy said.

A feeling of foreboding snaked through Jo's body. She hurried forward.

A horrifying sight met her eyes. The girls had gotten into the glue pot, and were patiently trying to glue together an assortment of books, papers, and scraps of fabric from Marmee's workbasket.

"Christopher Columbus!" Jo exclaimed. "Stop that this instant!"

Lucy dropped her hands.

"It's not our fault," Bettina said in a rush.

"Miss March?" Lucy said.

Jo's hands went to her hips. She turned to Bettina. "Then whose fault, pray tell, is it?"

"Yours," Bettina answered calmly.

"Miss March?" Lucy said again.

Bettina pouted. "You told us to amuse ourselves."

"Indeed, I did. But what made you think that gluing my family's things together was an acceptable game?" Jo asked sternly.

Bettina's face grew red. "How were we to know that we weren't supposed to touch these boring little trinkets?"

Boring little trinkets! Jo had been struggling to hold to her temper, but the slight to her family's meager possessions was too much to bear.

"Why, you wretched creature!" she snapped, advancing on Bettina. "You knew very well what you were doing! You deliberately misbehaved!"

Bettina's face grew redder. "No one speaks to me like that!" she cried. Tears welled up in her button eyes. "Your sister is nice and you're *mean!*"

"Miss March!" Lucy's voice was now a shout. "I think I glued my hands to the chair! She burst into tears, which only made Bettina wail louder. With a sigh, Jo crouched down next to the girls. She tried to wipe Bettina's tears with her apron, but the girl shrank back.

"It's dirty!"

"Don't worry, Lucy," Jo said over the girl's wails.

"I glued my finger to the table this morning, and it came right off. See?"

Jo held up her finger in front of Lucy's face, but the girl only wailed louder.

Then, another sob added to the din. Amy stood in the doorway. Her pretty face was puckered up, as though she'd been trying not to cry for so long that she couldn't stand it anymore.

"Amy, what's wrong?" Leaving Lucy's side, Jo hurried to her sister.

"Oh, Jo, I've been completely *degradaded*," Amy sobbed. "Teacher praised my drawing, and I was so happy. But all the way home, the girls teased me. Especially Jenny Snow. She called me 'teacher's pet' and said I was proud. I'm not proud, except for my drawing, for Jo, it really was quite good," Amy finished with a fresh sob.

"Of course it was, petal," Jo said, stroking her sister's golden hair.

"But Jenny said Teacher only feels sorry for me because I'm poor." Amy broke out into hiccups.

"She—*hic*—said that—*hic*—I should be ashamed to get special—*hic*—treatment just because I'm—*hic*—needy! Then Katy Brown threw a very icy *hic*—snowball at me and knocked off my bonnet! Oh, Jo!"

Hearing Amy's hiccuping sobs, the King girls took the opportunity to cry even louder. They wanted to regain Jo's attention, but Jo's concern for her sister had quickly grown to fury.

"Where are those girls now, dear?" Jo asked, trying to keep her voice soothing.

"They followed me—*hic*—home," Amy said, wiping at her wet, cold cheeks.

"Stay here, Amy," Jo ordered with tight lips. Apron flying, she raced out the door.

CHAPTER FIVE

Jo to the Rescue

J o hurried as fast as she could down the snowy
lane. Her hair fell out of its net and her apron strings
streamed out behind her. The cold air failed to cool
her warm cheeks and her hot temper.

All the frustrations of the morning seemed to
ball up into a fist inside her. She hated injustice. For
those mean girls to torment sweet Amy was just too
much to bear!

She reached the end of the lane and scanned
the street. Down by a spreading oak tree, Amy's

schoolmates lingered. Half sliding, half running, Jo made her way down the walk.

Five puzzled and increasingly nervous faces turned toward her as Jo charged toward them. She gave a final bound and slid into the tree. Her hand slapped against the broad trunk to steady herself.

"How dare you treat Amy that way!" Jo began breathlessly. "She's a sweet girl with a kind nature, which is more than I can say for your hard hearts! You torment her out of jealousy and mean-spiritedness, and I won't stand for it, do you hear?"

Snow flew as Jo stamped her foot. Five faces stared at her with round eyes. Five mouths dropped open. Too late, Jo realized that she must look a fright, with her soiled apron and her hair streaming out of its pins. A tiny scrap of newspaper flew out of her hair. The wind gently wafted it away.

Jo heard footsteps as Amy came puffing up behind her and tugged at her hand. "Please stop, Jo," she pleaded in a small voice. "Come back to the house."

"But I have more to say to these wretched girls." Jo stared down five pairs of eyes. The girls' gazes dropped, and they studied their boots. "You should be ashamed of yourselves," Jo scolded.

"Now, please, Jo," Amy begged. She yanked on Jo's hand.

"Oh, all right," Jo muttered. "I said my piece, I suppose."

Jo reluctantly allowed herself to be pulled away. But as the two sisters struggled down the icy walk, a cool voice trailed after them.

"Maybe we *should* feel sorry for Amy March, just as Teacher does," Jenny Snow trilled triumphantly. "After all, the poor thing has such a mean, horrible sister!"

Amy kept her lips pressed tightly together on the short walk back to the house. As soon as they entered, she primly removed her bonnet and cloak and regally crossed the hall toward the parlor.

"Oh, dear," Jo said to herself. "I suppose I've embarrassed Amy. But she can be such a sensitive thing!"

Then Jo remembered her two young charges. She hurried into the dining room, her heart in her throat. What fresh catastrophe did Bettina and Lucy have time to create?

But to Jo's relief, she saw that Meg had returned. Her sister had already soothed Bettina's tears with a cool cloth. Meg had even been able to unstick Lucy's little hands from the chair.

But Meg's expression was not as patient when she saw Jo. She hurriedly crossed the room toward her.

"Jo!" Meg admonished her in a whisper. "How could you have left the girls alone like that!"

"I'm sorry, Meg, truly," Jo said. "But Amy arrived in such a state. I had to defend her!"

"I wish you hadn't," Amy called tearfully from the parlor. "You just made things worse!"

Just then Beth entered the room. She had come in through the kitchen door and was still wearing her bonnet and cloak.

"Jo?" she asked. "Is everything all right?"

"Not nearly," Jo said with a sigh. "What's the matter, Beth?"

"Well, I covered the rest of the jams," Beth said timidly. "But I suppose you forgot to soak the saucepan. I'm afraid it may be ruined."

Meg tried to gather up the newspapers, but they were stuck to the table. "What's this?" she asked crossly.

Helplessness washed over Jo. She had let everyone down and could blame no one but herself. She wanted to tell her sisters she was sorry. She wanted to throw up her arms and holler in frustration. Feeling like the jam pots on the verge of bubbling over, Jo did the only thing she could. . . .

She rushed from the room, slamming the door behind her.

What a dreadful day, Jo wrote in her journal. She lay curled up on the old sofa in the garret. She had already wept her tears into the threadbare arm.

And the worst of it is, it's all my fault. Isn't that always the worst of it, somehow? All the defects of my character seemed to alight on my shoulder today. Impatience, carelessness, and a quick temper. When will I learn how to tame my own bad nature?

Sighing, Jo chewed on her pen. It was always easier when she wrote about her feelings. Getting all that confusion down on paper made it all clearer, somehow.

Now I see how selfish it was for me to complain yesterday. As if my sisters' burdens are any lighter than my own! Meg's little charges are difficult and tiring, to say the least. Beth's housework takes more care and patience than I realized. And poor Amy's schoolmates would a be a trial for a saint!

My sisters deserve a better sister, and a more cheer-ful companion.

Jo sighed. She placed her journal and pen back on the desk. Then she threw off the quilt and stood up.

"It's time I worked myself up to apologize," she told herself sternly. "Not to mention straighten up the mess I made downstairs!"

Jo crept down the stairs. On the way she met Hannah, who chuckled when she saw her.

"Now, don't you fret, Miss Jo. Your sisters took care of that mess. The glue is cleaned up and the table is scrubbed and oiled. The hearth got swept, and the jams are labeled. And a bit of baking soda shined up the saucepan, too."

"Oh, Hannah," Jo said. "I made a dreadful mess of things today, didn't I?"

"Let's just say that you do keep life interesting, dearie," Hannah said with a broad smile. Her thick hands patted Jo's shoulders. "Now straighten your collar and go see your sisters. They're in the parlor."

Jo walked down the stairs with a lighter step. Things must be gloomy in the parlor, she thought. Any one person's black mood always affected the family. Until apologies were offered and events laughed over, no one felt comfortable.

A sincere apology would jolly up her girls in no time.

But Jo paused at the parlor door, surprised. She'd heard the lighthearted peal of Meg's laugh. She caught the words "glue pot."

"Poor Jo," Meg said merrily. "Forced to face jam-making, housekeeping, and the King girls, all in one morning!"

"Yes, I'm afraid she was overwhelmed," Beth said.

Amy giggled. "I just hope we don't all spread glue on our toast one morning!"

Another peal of laughter came through the door. Jo leaned against it, suddenly feeling queer.

How strange that the three girls were laughing at her behind her back! It seemed to Jo that they were *enjoying* the idea of her string of catastrophes! She'd had a perfectly dreadful time, and it had been for their amusement.

Jo's imagination sparked. Why had a string of catastrophes occurred on the same day in the first place? It was decidedly odd. Especially since only yesterday Jo had remarked that Meg, Beth, and Amy's paths were smoother than hers!

Suspicions crowded Jo's brain. Why had Meg brought the King girls here? She could have taken them back to their own home. And why had Amy been so upset over some name-calling and a snow-ball? Usually, her sister was better able to bear such things. And even her dear Beth hadn't warned her that she was going to leave her with the jam-making! Had she deliberately not told Jo, knowing that such a chore would add another bother to Jo's day? Had they all arranged to teach Jo a lesson?

"I'm not sure I would have blamed Jo if she had glued little Bettina's fingers to the table," Meg said, laughter bubbling underneath her words.

"She certainly was provoked," Beth said, and the three girls chuckled again.

Jo's heart beat fast and her face flushed. Usually, she didn't mind being laughed at if she deserved it. But she liked to be the one to start the merriment, not be left out of it!

CHAPTER SIX

Betrayed!

I can't imagine my sweet sisters playing such a trick. Then again, they were extremely provoked. I suppose I can be a trial to them at times. When I get in a state, I seem to be incapable of holding my tongue. But it's one thing to scrap or fuss at each other, and quite another to play such a mean trick. I simply don't believe that they would do such a thing. It's just an odd fancy of mine.

Jo peeked over the top of her journal at her family. They looked the same as usual. It was evening, close to nine o'clock, and the fire was dying. Marmee was just finishing a letter to Father at the desk. Soon she would beckon them, and they would gather round the old piano and sing before climbing the stairs to bed.

Beth's head drooped over the socks she was knitting for the soldiers' Christmas baskets. Amy was daydreaming, her work in her lap. And Meg was examining a blue sock she had just finished, holding it up to the light.

Nothing was different. The scene was full of sweet peace and family contentment. A smile stole over Jo's face as her gaze swept over the sweet, quiet sisters she loved so. Then she bent over her journal again.

I am leaping to the wrong conclusion, as I so often do. My writer's imagination is a gift, no doubt, but oh, it can be a curse at times! Thank heavens I've come to my senses!

Marmee looked up from her desk. "It's time, girls. Beth? Shall we have a song before bed?"

Beth rubbed her sleepy eyes and rose to her feet. Her fingers danced across the old, chipped keys of the piano. "What shall I play tonight?" she asked as her sisters rose to join her. " 'Home, Sweet Home?' "

" 'Listen to the Mockingbird!' " Amy suggested. It was her favorite song.

Meg leafed through Beth's music. "How about 'Sweet Blackberry Jam?' "

Jo froze as the word "jam" hung in the air. She saw her sisters exchange glances that reeked of guilt. Beth looked worried, Amy mischievous, and merriment brightened Meg's eyes. She pressed her lips together as if trying to restrain her laugh. A giggle escaped Amy, and Meg stepped on her foot.

Beth hurriedly played the opening notes of "Home Sweet Home." Jo stood behind her sisters, but the words of the familiar air seemed to stick in her throat.

Her heart burned as she remembered the laughter behind the parlor door. She'd been right. Her sisters had tricked her!

Amy handed her a scone dripping with sweet butter. But when Jo bit into it, the butter turned into glue. She tried to spit the scone out, but her lips were suddenly fused together. She couldn't open her jaw!

In a panic, she looked over at Amy and Meg. They began to laugh. Their eyes gleamed like dark buttons.

Beth pointed at her. "Her apron is dirty!"
Meg nodded. "She's an inferior! Be nice!"
Help me, *Jo tried to say. But she could not open*
her mouth.

Jo woke. She sat upright in bed, gasping for air.
Her heart pounded so hard that it seemed as though
it would leap out of her chest.

Jo wiggled her jaw gratefully. She took deep
breaths, trying to calm herself.

"It was only a dream," she murmured, shivering.
"Only a dream."

The sky outside was full of heavy clouds. Jo saw
a few flakes twinkle down past her dark window.
She put on her stocking cap and slippers. Then she
opened her trunk and took out her manuscript. Tonight she would finish it. No matter if she had to
write until dawn! No matter if her heart hurt from
the idea of the treachery of her sisters. . . .

Treachery . . . now there was a highly dramatic word.

The idea burst upon Jo's brain at that instant.
She knew how to make the story work!

Her brain teemed with ideas as she crept up
the garret stairs. Events fell into place. Scenes were
expanded; scenes were dropped. Suddenly "The Cas-

tle of Deceit" fell into place, exactly as she'd hoped it would.

In one flash she'd seen what she had to do. It would require just one major change. She would make the three brothers into three sisters!

Now all she had to do was write it.

Up in the garret, she pulled the quilts around her. She skimmed through the pages excitedly.

With a stroke of the pen, Quentin, Raymundo, and Horatio became Miranda, Beatrice, and Amaryllis. And the brave and valiant Delano became the innocent but resourceful heroine, Dove. Instead of being evil, the count became Dove's sweetheart. She hadn't needed another villain, anyway. What had she been thinking of? She gave all the count's evil deeds to Miranda, the oldest of the girls.

Once she'd made that decision, the story flowed under Jo's fingertips as though the pen moved without her pushing it. She had never cast females as the villains before. It added a new verve to her writing. Jo's eyes gleamed as she wrote, her pen flying across the paper.

Her hurt feelings of the day also helped to push her pen. Jo's pain made her write with a special fire.

The three wicked sisters were closely modeled on her own. Miranda was pretty and had great dignity, as Meg did. Beatrice was rather shy, like Beth, and Jo even gave her a pet cat she was fond of. And Amaryllis was artistic. Jo took Amy's small vanities and exaggerated them, making Amaryllis a conceited girl who was constantly patting her blond curls.

And how could she help making Dove tall and chestnut-haired and fond of writing, like herself? Jo made sure to add superior fencing skills as well.

Her stormy tale gained fire and flash. The three sisters plotted and deceived in order to defraud poor Dove of her fortune. And Dove responded with courage and a plucky refusal to yield.

It was close to dawn when Jo finally recopied the last page of the manuscript. She put down her pen, her eyes heavy.

"Well, that's done," she said aloud. She looked around the empty garret, but of course there was no one to applaud her victory. Jo smothered the pang of excitement in a yawn.

She carried the manuscript downstairs and placed it carefully in her trunk. Tomorrow she would mail it to Mr. Pillson, the editor of the *Patriot Gazette*.

But now her bed looked inviting. She slipped under the cold sheets and shivered, hoping her body would warm soon. Within seconds she was fast asleep.

It seemed she had barely closed her eyes before Meg was shaking her awake.

"Jo," Meg said crossly. "If you're not ill, you have to wake up properly. I can't be shaking you every morning. I'll be late to get to the King's. Everyone is already at breakfast."

"Sorry," Jo said thickly. She looked over at her trunk. The hasp was open. She must have forgotten to close it last night.

The ice-cold water in her basin revived her. Jo dressed quickly and hurried downstairs.

Everyone was running a bit late that morning. Marmee had left the house early to tend to a sick friend. Without her gentle reminders, the morning had not gone smoothly. Amy had forgotten to tie her pinafore, and had tripped on the stairs. Beth had let the tea steep too long, and it tasted bitter. And no one had remembered to fetch the sugar.

"I've been back and forth to the kitchen three times already," Meg said with a sigh.

"I got the napkins," Amy pointed out.

"I'll get the sugar," Jo offered, hurrying to the kitchen. Now that she was awake, she felt a guilty pang when she thought of her manuscript. Doubts crowded her mind. Perhaps she was being hasty. The choice of the song last night could have been a coincidence. Just because her sisters had looked guilty and tried not to laugh didn't mean they'd played a joke on her.

"Here we are, sweets for my sweet sisters," Jo said, placing the sugar on the table with a bright smile.

But no answering smiles met hers. The cold, gray morning made everyone feel grumpy.

"I don't know how I shall face my friends today," Amy mumbled into her porridge.

"The King house is sure to be in an uproar after the ball last night," Meg said with a sigh. "And the girls will still be in a state because of yesterday. They both like to hold grudges."

Jo stirred her tea, her lips tight. Were Amy and Meg deliberately reminding her of her mistakes yesterday?

"I think Aunt March is better, Jo," Beth said softly. "You might have it easier today, at least. Hannah left some broth for you to take to her."

"Just don't take the glue pot," Amy said with a smirk.

"Amy, don't tease," Beth said. "Poor Jo had such a bad time yesterday."

Poor Jo! Jo swallowed her tea hastily. Now they felt sorry for her! Was it because they felt guilty about what they'd done?

"Hurry, Jo," Meg urged. "We're late."

Bonnet. Gloves. Scarf. Coat. Jo donned her outdoor gear thoughtfully. Around the corner in the hall, she could hear Meg helping Amy into her coat and scarf.

"Do stop provoking Jo, will you, Amy?" Meg murmured.

Jo moved closer to the door and strained to hear.

"But it is all so amusing, Meg!" Amy whispered. "The jam, and the glue, and the King girls, and everything all at once—"

"I know, dear, but we've had our fun," Meg said. "Reminding Jo will only make her cross."

Jo tied her bonnet strings with a jerk. *We've had our fun.* She was right! They *had* played a joke on her!

Jo didn't say a word as she and Meg walked briskly down the lane to the main road. Meg didn't seem to notice. Obviously, she didn't care that she'd broken her sister's heart!

"Goodbye, Jo," Meg said hurriedly as they

reached the corner. "I hope everything goes better today!"

"Goodbye, Meg," Jo said sternly. She wheeled and stalked down the road. But instead of heading right to Aunt March's, Jo stopped at the post office.

She was already late. What did a few more minutes matter?

She placed the bundle in the postmaster's hands. Biting her lip, she watched him put it into a box marked "Boston." She headed back out into the winter morning, feeling another twinge of guilt. She had drawn her sisters' characters so accurately! Had she gone too far?

But remembering what they'd done made Jo's resolve harden. They had tricked her, laughed at her, and then pitied her. Just like the sisters in "The Castle of Deceit"!

CHAPTER SEVEN

Duties and Pleasures

"You're late!" Aunt March announced as Jo made her hasty way into the sitting room of Plumfield, Aunt March's grand old house. She hadn't even stopped to remove her outdoor things.

"I'm sorry, Aunt," Jo said in the meekest voice she could muster. She didn't want to inflame Aunt March's temper today, of all days. Her nerves felt so strained she feared she'd fly at Aunt March with unforgivable fury before the day was through.

Aunt March pointed a long, crooked finger at her.

"Thought you could pass me off to your sister, did you?" she cackled.

"Certainly not, Aunt March," Jo replied, unwinding her scarf from her head, where it had tied down her bonnet in the stiff wind. "I know you'd miss my odd ways far too much."

Aunt March laughed, so she must have been feeling better. "Pride, girl! That's your problem! It's pride! Pride and temper. Well, I saved plenty of things for you to do. Fetch me another cup of tea, and we'll read the Boston papers."

Jo hurried to take off her things. As she passed by the cage of Aunt March's parrot, Polly, the bird let out a squawk.

"Temper, temper!" Polly brayed. Then she imitated Aunt March's cackling laugh.

"Quiet, or I'll fry you up for lunch, you tough old bird," Jo whispered.

"What was that, Josephine?" Aunt March called.

"I just called Polly a dear old bird," Jo said, hurrying out of the room.

She made her way to the kitchen, where she told the cook to make up a tea tray. Jo fetched the china and the linen napkin, thinking of the parrot's harsh cry.

Temper! Even a bird could detect her biggest fault!

Jo smoothed the napkin and filled the sugar bowl. Weeks ago, Marmee had spoken to her about her need to control her temper. "Unless you meditate and pray on it, your temper will continue to rule you," Marmee had said in her gentle way.

How she longed to be gentle and good, like Marmee! But it took such an effort. Sometimes Jo felt like a kettle on the boil. And a kettle had to whistle once it was filled with steam, didn't it?

"Oh, dear." Jo sighed under her breath as she placed a rose on Aunt March's tea tray. "I suppose I should be like Marmee and forgive and forget others' wrongs. But it's so difficult—I'm so often in the right!"

That day Jo doubled her effort to be patient and kind with Aunt March. She fetched and carried and read aloud in a soothing voice. She arranged flowers, footstools, and shawls. Although she was bone-tired from her sleepless night, her energy never flagged.

But as she called up every ounce of goodness for her aunt, she could not seem to spare any for her sisters. Jo did as Marmee told her. She meditated on the wrongs done to her. She circled the situation from every side. But try as she might, she could not seem to forgive them. No matter how she tried.

Jo trudged home through the early December darkness. She felt cross and tired, and she had a headache. At home chores awaited her. There would be the fire to kindle, the tea table to set, and the food to bring. As Marmee's work kept her out till after dusk, the March girls began tea without her.

There would be an overflowing workbasket for Jo to tend to—soldiers' socks to knit and button-holes to sew. All she wanted to do was sink into the sofa and close her eyes.

She knocked the snow off her boots on the stoop. She opened the door and tore at the wet knot in her bonnet strings. Then she heard the sound of a suppressed giggle from the parlor.

"Probably still laughing at me," Jo decided sourly as she wrestled with the knot. Finally she tore the bonnet off her head in frustration. She hung it up along with her coat.

But when she opened the parlor door, a wonderful sight met her eyes.

The table was pulled up close to the fire. It was already set with the best linen and china. She was sure she smelled Hannah's cinnamon buns. And were those chocolates gleaming on a silver tray?

"Surprise!"

Meg, Beth, and Amy popped out from behind the sofa and chairs. Then Teddy Laurence jumped out from behind the curtain. Everyone laughed at the thunderstruck expression on Jo's face.

Laurie was the first to recover. He put on a dignified expression and pulled out a chair. Then, he gave his deepest, most polite bow. "The guest of honor has arrived," he announced.

CHAPTER EIGHT

Sweet Forgiveness

"*D*on't look so alarmed, Jo," Laurie said. His black eyes twinkled at her from across the room. "You'll notice there's no jam on the table."

Jo tensed. Her sisters had already told Laurie all about her string of disasters! Had he laughed at her, too?

But Meg hurried forward to lead Jo to her seat. "Don't be wicked about Jo's day, Laurie, for it was all her sisters' fault."

"I'm afraid so," Beth agreed.

Stunned, Jo fell into her seat. "It was?"

Beth's gentle smile beamed at Jo. "I should have told you ahead of time about the jam-making. It wasn't a very restful day for you, was it?"

"And I never should have left you with those King girls," Meg said, as Jo looked at her sisters in a daze. "I know what horrors they can be with a stranger. I should have at least given you an idea of what would please them and keep them quiet."

"That's right," Amy said, hastily swallowing the chocolate she'd snitched. "You were quite right to fly at those girls, Jo. They were dreadfully cruel to me. And thanks to you, now I know who my *true* friends are. Why, Katy Brown said she was sorry she threw that snowball. And besides, real friends don't *ostrich-size* you."

A sober-faced Laurie examined Amy's curls.

"What are you doing, Laurie?" Amy asked.

"Searching for feathers," Laurie said. "Didn't you say *ostrich*?"

The girls all laughed. "That's *ostracize*, dear, and no one here shall be excluded from the feast," Meg said. "As I told Amy this morning, we couldn't help laughing yesterday at the disasters, but Jo had to endure them, and she needs a little comfort as a reward."

SWEET FORGIVENESS

Jo felt a rush of affection that brought tears to her eyes. She'd been so wrong! She smiled at all her sisters and patted Beth's hand.

"This is a jolly surprise, all of you. I can't tell you how much it means to me, especially considering how beastly I've been."

"Hannah made the buns especially for you," Beth said. "And Laurie brought the chocolates. I left a note for him in the P.O. that you needed some cheer."

The "P.O." was the mailbox that Laurie had placed in the hedge between their two properties. Letters, parcels, and little gifts passed back and forth between the two houses. The box was rarely empty.

But suddenly the mention of the "P.O." struck Jo with remorse and horror. This morning she had mailed off the manuscript! Oh, why hadn't she waited until her temper had cooled!

"And I volunteered to help in the mission to jolly up Jo," Laurie put in.

Jo squeezed her sister's hand. "You are my angel, Bethy," she said in a choked voice.

Laurie looked hurt. "What about me? I brought the chocolates."

"You're too naughty to be an angel, Teddy. Particularly now that you're hoarding those buns," Jo said, attempting a laugh.

Laurie handed her the plate with mock cere-mony. "I say, a fellow can't get a spot of praise from you hard-hearted March girls without having to beg for it. Shall I go down on bended knee?"

"We praise you all the time, Laurie, and well you know it. And you're frightfully spoiled because of it, too," Meg said decidedly.

She began to pour the tea with a dignified air. Amy crooked her finger as she drank, trying to look grown up and graceful. Beth smiled at Jo across the teacups, and Laurie heaped so many cinnamon buns on Jo's plate that they all burst out laughing again.

Warmed by the fire and the affection, Jo took a sip of hot tea and felt her confusion vanish. Her sisters' love surrounded her in a close circle. Forgive-ness tasted as sweet as Hannah's cinnamon buns. For the time being, she pushed the thought of the manuscript from her mind. Why, it hadn't even reached the newspaper office yet. She had time to send a letter withdrawing it. Then she could rewrite it. And still in time for Christmas!

"You're the best sisters in the world," Jo told them in a burst of warmth. "And the best friend," she added to Laurie, who made a show of sinking to his knees with clasped hands.

Merry laughter bubbled up once again. Buns were passed, stories and jokes were told, and the teatime hour seemed over in minutes.

Laurie rose with a reluctant glance at the clock. "I'm sorry to report that my Latin studies await," he said ruefully. "Thank you, ladies, for a most delicious tea."

"Thank you for the chocolates and the roses," Beth said with an appreciative glance at the bright yellow bouquet.

Promising a "rip-roaring party of my own soon," Laurie left. The three sisters sat back with a combined *oof* and stared at the crumbs on their plates.

Jo rose. "I'll wash everything—don't move. It's only fair."

"It's all right," Meg said, springing up.

Beth picked up Amy's plate and her own. "If we all work, it will go faster."

Meg stationed herself at the sink. Jo turned the clearing of the table into a parade, with Beth and Amy waving china and silver on the way to the kitchen. Soon the table was cleared, the cloth swept free of crumbs, and the dishes washed and put away.

Meg's cheeks were rosy from the steam when she turned from the sink to Jo.

"I nearly forgot!" she cried. "Your present!"

"My word," Jo said, taken aback. "How extraordinary. If parties and presents are my reward, I shall be a moody, unpleasant shrew more often!"

"Come into the parlor," Meg told her, drying her hands and laughing. "I'll fetch it."

Jo returned to the parlor and in a moment heard Meg's light step approaching. Meg's arms were full of Jo's burgundy gown.

"I remade it again," she told her.

She held it up for Jo's inspection. Instead of the ruffle, there was now a sweet, simple ribbon running around the hem, and an edging of delicate lace.

"Meg, it's beautiful!" Jo exclaimed. She gave her sister a heartfelt hug, crushing the dress. "What a neat, pretty border. But to do all that work—"

"Do you truly like it?"

"It is exactly what I should wish for," Jo said. "It suits me, and it's handsome, too. Thank you." She squeezed Meg's shoulders again.

"You're quite welcome," Meg said, satisfied. "And I shall never try to 'ruffle you up' again."

"Marmee will be home soon," Beth remarked.

"I'll build up the fire," Jo said, hurrying for the poker.

"Where are her slippers?" Amy wondered.

"I have them," Beth said. "Where is the evening paper?" She looked under a cushion.

Jo put another log on the fire and poked it into position. Behind her, she enjoyed hearing the usual cheerful bustle of the girls making the room cozy for Marmee. She whistled a tune.

She expected Meg to scold her for whistling in such a boyish fashion. But instead, Meg said to Amy in a low tone, "It looks as though our wounded dove has mended and is singing again."

Jo's whistle died in a soft breath. *Dove?* That was the name of her character in "The Castle of Deceit"!

Under normal circumstances, Jo would have turned around and said, "yes, because your dove is stuffed with chocolates," or some such sally. Instead, she kept her face to the fire and listened.

Ears burning, she heard Amy giggle and whisper: "Another day and we should have been tempted to lock her in the garret."

Lock her in the garret! That was what the three stepsisters did to poor Dove!

Despite the fire, Jo's blood ran cold. Suddenly all her pleasure dissolved into fresh suspicions.

What if she had been right? And what if Meg had read her manuscript while she was sleeping? Had she told her sisters about their portrayals in "The Castle of Deceit"?

And was this tea party an elaborate joke on Jo? Was it a trick to soften her nature enough to rewrite her story? If so, it had been a clever ruse. After all it had almost worked!

CHAPTER NINE

The Thorn

I mustn't jump and think the worst, Jo wrote in her journal that evening.

I know my faults so well—we have had such a long acquaintance! I have a way of flying about and leaping to conclusions. So I will be careful and go over the facts calmly. I must let their behavior be my guide. And I must remember my sisters' good natures— and my own.

Jo was stern with herself. She told herself that
her sisters' attempt to "jolly her up" wasn't a sinister
plot out of a story. She reminded herself that she'd
often left the hasp open on her trunk. It didn't mean
that Meg would peek at her manuscript!

And she told herself that Meg was cross with
her that morning because Jo had made her late—
not because she'd been portrayed as the wicked
Miranda.

She told herself all of these things. And she
desperately wanted to believe them.

Here is the dreadful thing, she wrote.

*If it is true that they have tricked me, it is no more
than I deserve. I am so often cross these days, and
indulge my moods with wild words and fancies. Perhaps I have been cross once too often. Only a trio of
angels would not be tempted to teach me a lesson!*

*So I should not blame my sisters . . . yet I do!
And I shall try to forget my suspicions . . . if I can!*

"Tell me every detail!" Amy burst out the next
afternoon, when Meg and Jo had returned from their
call on the Moffat girls.

"What did Annie wear? Did she wear ribbons in

her hair, or a net? Is the house very fine?" Questions tumbled from Amy's lips faster than the girls could possibly answer them.

Jo lowered herself to the sofa and angled her boots toward the fire.

"All I can say is that everything I saw in that parlor was tasseled or fringed," she said, "from sofas to pillows to chairs to gowns to shawls. I was surprised the cake itself wasn't covered in silk fringe, and that tassels didn't hang from the teacups!"

Beth laughed and Marmee smiled, but Amy continued to press Meg for details.

"Did you see Belle?" she asked, naming Annie Moffat's elegant older sister.

"She arrived as we were leaving," Meg told her with a sigh. "She was all in blue velvet, and looked like a dream. She wore the most cunning bonnet—"

"Tipped over one eye, as though she'd hit her head on a low branch," Jo interrupted with a grin.

"It looked charming," Meg insisted. "And oh, Amy, if only you could have seen Belle's pearls! They were an engagement gift from her future mother-in-law."

"If only we had them for our theatricals," Jo said, reaching for her workbasket. "We could *truly* play pirates." She squinted one eye and flourished her knitting needle at Beth. "Avast ye, matey!"

The girls all laughed at Jo's fierce expression. But Amy sighed.

"If *I* had a necklace of pearls, I would die in peace," she said dramatically.

"Clutching them round your neck, I expect," Meg said, amused.

Jo froze. There it was again! Amaryllis, Amy's character, had died clutching her pearls!

Jo bent her head over her knitting. She felt her ears burn. Try as she might to forget her suspicions, they had returned in a rush. First, Meg had called her "Dove." Amy had joked about locking her in the garret. Now Amy and Meg were talking of pearls! The coincidences were piling up.

Jo had neglected her workbasket while working on her story. Now she saw the piles of socks and scarves the other girls had already completed for the soldiers' Christmas baskets. She compared their efforts to her own, and was ashamed.

So that evening Jo concentrated on her knitting. Brave soldiers shouldn't have to freeze that winter because of her own poor spirits!

Even as she worked, a tiny thorn pricked Jo's

generous heart. She wanted to pluck it out but was unable to. She hoped that by working hard and saying nothing it would work its way out, the way a splinter sometimes will from an injured finger.

But worry made her fingers slow, and her eyes were tired from her long weeks of writing late at night. Jo felt more behind than ever.

So once again Jo woke herself at midnight and trudged her weary way up the garret stairs. Instead of her manuscript, she brought her workbasket. She knit into the morning hours, keeping herself awake by singing or whistling. When she could barely focus on the work in her hands, she allowed herself to go to bed.

The next few days passed in a fog. She managed to do all her work, but it was a listless, strange Jo who tended to Aunt March, set the tea table, knitted socks for soldiers.

They're used to my odd ways, so no doubt they think I'm working on a story, Jo thought. That would explain how silent I've been. And I do try to be cheerful!

But it was hard to go on when the thorn pricked her, and her heart was sore.

*   *   *

Meg shivered as she pulled the curtains wider to let in the last of the afternoon sun's weak rays.

"The days are shorter and shorter," she said. "These early twilights make me feel so cold and damp and hopeless, somehow—like being shut up in a dungeon."

Jo bit her lip. That was how Miranda met her fate—shut up in a dungeon by Dove and her sweetheart, Count Leander. Another coincidence! Could there be any doubt that her sisters were tormenting her?

"If Christmas didn't come in December, it would be a sorry month," Amy agreed.

"I have an early Christmas present for you, Amy, just to cheer you up," Beth said. She rose and placed a paper chain around Amy's neck. "Your pearls, madam."

Amy clapped her hands, and Meg laughed. "How clever!" Meg cried.

"They are lovely," Amy said, holding them out to examine them. "Look, Jo."

Jo forced her lips to smile. Were they teasing her? Well, if so, she would rather die than let them see it. "Now you're a grand lady," she said.

"Fit for a castle," Meg said, smiling.

With a strangled cry, Jo rose.

"Jo?" Beth asked. "Is anything wrong?"

"Something in my throat," Jo muttered, hurrying away.

As she passed into the hall, she saw that the mail had arrived. Hannah had left it on the pewter plate by the door. Jo leafed through the envelopes, hoping for a letter from Father. That would cheer her, no matter what her mood.

Instead, she found a thin envelope addressed to her. It was from Mr. Pillson, the Boston publisher of the *Patriot Gazette*.

With trembling fingers, Jo slit open the envelope. When she unfolded the letter, a check fell out. She'd sold the story!

Quickly, Jo scanned the letter. She was too flustered to take it in. Phrases swam up at her: *. . . delighted to publish 'The Castle of Deceit' . . . if there are any more stories you care to submit in the same vein . . . the use of female villains was a bold stroke. . . .*

Jo folded up the letter. The flare of excitement she'd felt had died as quickly as it had been born. It was as though someone had thrown a wet blanket over a blazing fire.

During all those long, cold nights in the garret, she had imagined this very moment. She'd dreamed about what she'd do. How she'd perhaps present the check on a plate to Marmee. How she'd show the letter to the girls. How she'd throw pebbles at Laurie's window, then announce that a celebrated authoress was coming to call.

But she didn't want to do any of those things.

Sick and sore at heart, Jo leaned against the wall. She told herself that her sisters deserved what she'd done. But still she could not feel any pleasure in her success.

Perhaps she could write to Mr. Pillson and tell him she wished to withdraw the story after all. She would enclose the check. She was tired of feeling cross and suspicious, and it was the only way to set her mind at rest. What was the money worth now, when it would not gladden her heart to spend it on her sisters?

Perhaps she should ask Marmee what to do. She longed for her mother's wise counsel. But then she'd have to confess her suspicions, and Marmee would question the girls, and the house would be in an uproar. No, it was better to keep silent.

Jo placed the rest of the mail on the tray and slipped the letter into her pocket. She entered the parlor unnoticed.

"I am quite serious, Amy," Beth was saying. "I hate the thought of all those geese and turkeys enjoying themselves this month. Getting fat on grain, not knowing how short their days truly are. It's simply cruel!"

Jo heard the words like a tolling bell. She had held out the hope that her Beth was not involved in the conspiracy against her.

Jo hadn't been able to bear killing off Beatrice. Instead, she had exiled her to an island, where she was poor and alone, but was given geese to tend.

Jo fingered the letter in her pocket. And to think she had considered withdrawing her story!

She hardened her heart. They had all betrayed her. She would never relent!

CHAPTER TEN

Second Thoughts

*I*t seemed harder than ever to rise from her bed that night. The house seemed colder, and the garret steps steeper. Jo didn't know how long she could keep this up. She'd never worked so long and so late before.

But her workbasket was still piled with items. She'd only been able to complete two pairs of socks, and Meg had done fifteen.

Yawning, Jo picked up her needles and began.

It was late when she heard a step on the stair.

Or had it been the wind? Jo paused and looked over her knitting as the garret door creaked open.

It was Marmee. She carried a candle high, and when she saw Jo, her face grew stern. Then she saw the knitting in Jo's hands, and it softened.

With quiet steps, she came and sat on the old sofa next to Jo.

"Your bed was empty," she said. "I was worried, Jo. You never work this late."

"Oh, Marmee, I know," Jo said. "But I was finishing up a story last week, and now I'm so behind." She gestured at the wool in her workbasket. "I just can't let you down. Or the poor soldiers."

"I see." Marmee picked up the tangled wool and began to wind it around her fingers to straighten it.

"Jo, I find this troubling. You're aware of how I feel about your staying up in this cold room half the night. Interrupted sleep and sitting in the cold invites illness. I know I allow you to work up here, but I expect you to come to bed at a decent hour. And I do not consider this a decent hour," Marmee ended firmly, placing the wool back in the basket.

"It's just that I got so behind—" Jo started.

"So you decided to risk your health and good temper?"

Jo sighed, and Marmee patted her hand. "Jo,

dear, sometimes I think that half your troubles spring from your impulsive generosity. I cannot reproach you for that. But it's your responsibility to organize your work during the daylight hours so that you don't need to do this. And if you need help, you have three sisters with willing hands."

At the mention of her sisters, Jo could not prevent a shadow from passing over her face. She ducked her head, hoping that Marmee wouldn't notice it.

"Haven't you realized," Marmee said softly, "that your short temper of late is due to these late hours? Without rest, our nerves fray."

Jo opened her mouth to protest. She wanted to tell Marmee that her short temper was entirely justified. But she hesitated.

"I'm sorry, Marmee," she said instead. "I promise I won't rise at midnight again."

But Marmee had noted the shadow and the hesitation, for she noted everything. She drew Jo against her shoulder and stroked her hair gently.

"I've seen your distance from your sisters, dear," she said. "You needn't tell me the cause if you don't wish to. But it's grieved my heart to see it."

"It's grieved my heart, too, Marmee," Jo said

brokenly. "I try to shoulder my burden, but it's so heavy this time."

"Oh, Jo," Marmee murmured, placing her cheek against the top of Jo's hair. "I'll not offer advice, except to point out one thing to you. Until you learn the difference between hurt and righteous anger, you'll have an unhappy heart."

Jo straightened so that she could look into Marmee's kind eyes. "What do you mean, Marmee?"

"You turn your hurt into anger," Marmee explained. "If you would just admit to yourself that your feelings are hurt and go about either accepting it, forgiving it, or changing it, you would get along better, Jo. Instead, you turn your hurt into a knot of anger and pride."

Jo swallowed. Marmee's words struck home.

"Your sisters are doing the best they can to keep their *own* tempers in the face of yours. Don't harbor a bitter heart, darling Jo. Can't you take your sisters back into your confidence and trust?"

Jo kept her head bent and her eyes on the knitting in her lap. She could not bear to meet Marmee's loving gaze.

"I don't know," she whispered.

*   *   *

The next evening Jo trudged home through the early twilight. Aunt March was feeling better, so she'd actually received callers today for a short period. That meant that Jo had had a half hour to herself. She had immediately ducked into the library to read. She had been able to get through exactly one paragraph before falling into a deep sleep, her cheek pressed into the binding of *Nicholas Nickleby*.

All day Jo had tried to meditate on her mother's words. But she was so tired.

"What I need is a good night's sleep," Jo told herself stoutly as she opened the front door. "Thanks to Marmee, I'll have one tonight at last."

But the thought of her overflowing workbasket and her many chores filled her with dismay. Jo removed her cloak and bonnet, straightened her shoulders, and entered the parlor.

"Jo, you're home at last," Beth called cheerfully.

"Isn't it beastly cold today?" Amy asked.

"Come by the fire," Meg urged.

All of her sisters had knitting in their hands. *Her* knitting, Jo saw. They had raided her workbasket!

Meg saw the knowledge dawn in Jo's face.

"Marmee told us how you've been staying up late to catch up," she told her. "I hope you don't mind, Jo."

"I'm almost on time with my work," Amy said. "So I thought I could help with yours."

"It's dreadful that you had to sneak out of bed at night," Beth said. "Why didn't you come to us sooner?"

"Tomorrow is Saturday, so Marmee told us to be quiet so you can sleep late," Amy told her. "Even I shall be quiet. I promised."

Jo leaned against the door frame, her knees feeling weak. Seeing her sisters with their heads bent over *her* work flooded her heart with love.

Jo hugged the feeling to her. It had been too long since she had felt this warmth in her chest— this deep, abiding love. How could she have swung the gates against it for even a minute, let alone for days? She had told herself to let their behavior be her guide, and now they had showed her how dear she was to them.

How could she have doubted the loyalty of those she loved best? How could she have forgotten the three most generous hearts in the world?

Where they loved and trusted freely, she had housed resentment and distrust. She had been distant and moody, and drove them to distraction. Still, when she needed help, they had offered it without her asking.

But what would happen to the sturdy love and trust she counted on when her story was published?

Jo's heart supplied the answer. They would go on loving her, she knew. They would forgive her. It was their nature to do so. But she would hurt them so badly. And she would embarrass them in front of everyone in Concord!

Jo's heart beat wildly. How could she have been such a fool?

But it wasn't too late. They must never know what a wretch she'd been. They must never be hurt by the fact that she'd suspected them.

She had to stop the publication of that story!

CHAPTER ELEVEN

A Mad Dash

Jo was allowed to sleep late the next day. Such a treat should have combined with her weariness and kept her abed until late in the morning.

But Jo awoke early, her mind already working. Before falling asleep, she had formed a desperate plan. A letter might go astray, or not reach the newspaper office in time. And it would not plead her case with the same force as an appearance. Today she must get to Boston!

She had three difficulties. First, such a trip required permission from Marmee. But if Jo asked permission, she would have to explain why she needed to go, and she couldn't face that. Second, she would need an escort, which was only proper. And third, she would need the fare.

She would have none of these things. And she would have to go, regardless.

Jo's face paled at the thought. But then she pictured Meg, Beth, and Amy reading her story in the paper and having to face all of Concord, and she knew she must do it.

She would have to count on luck. Perhaps a kindly farmer would give her a ride in his cart. Boston was twenty miles away. She'd walk if she had to! Once there, she'd have a better chance of finding a ride home.

Jo dressed hurriedly and dashed downstairs. Meg was in the kitchen, preparing breakfast with Hannah.

"Jo! What are you doing?" Meg scolded. "You're supposed to stay in bed this morning as long as you like. I was planning on bringing you a hot cup of tea as a treat."

"Bless you, that's sounds like heaven, but I can't lie in bed so long," Jo said, trying to sound cheery.

"Marmee already left for church to plan the social," Meg said. "So it's just four for breakfast."

"I must take some of these muffins over to the Laurence house," Hannah said, placing a basket over her arm. "I know how much the old gentleman loves them."

Meg and Jo exchanged secret smiles. Everyone knew that Hannah was bringing the muffins for the young gentleman, not the old one. Hannah dearly loved to spoil Laurie, but would rather die than admit it.

The door banged behind Hannah. Meg began to slice apples, her dark head bent over the task.

"Jo, I didn't tell you what Marmee said to all of us yesterday," she said. "She told us that when a sister is troubled and her temper is short, we need to work harder to keep our own. I know she was talking directly to me, though she didn't say it." Meg looked up, her eyes contrite. "I'm sorry I was cross with you, Jo."

Jo hugged Meg. "You weren't a bit cross, so please don't apologize," she said, her heart full.

Meg leaned against her tall sister for a moment. Then she straightened as the kettle began to boil. "I'll make the tea."

"I'll set the table," Jo announced, picking up four plates.

When she walked into the dining room, Beth was already arranging a single rose in a vase. "Jo! What are you doing awake?" she asked, disappointed. "I was going to bring you a tray!"

"I had a lovely night's sleep, and I'm back to myself again, I hope," Jo said, smiling at Beth tenderly.

Beth ducked her head as she stroked the flower with a delicate finger. "Jo, Marmee spoke to us yesterday about keeping our hearts light and watching out for each other. I know she was talking to me. I should have noticed how burdened you were. I'm so sorry I didn't see it."

"Oh, Beth." Jo felt her eyes sting. No one could touch her heart more tenderly than sweet Beth. "You are an angel. Everything was my fault. You don't know how dreadful I am."

"You are my own Jo," Beth said, smiling. "And you're perfect."

Yawning, Amy entered the dining room. She stopped when she saw Jo. "Oh, this *is* unfair!" she cried. "I thought you were in your room, Jo! And I was going to bring you up some apples and cheese, just what you say a simple breakfast should be."

"Dear Amy, Hannah made muffins, so I shall have a treat just the same," Jo said, setting the plates around the table.

Beth went off to fetch napkins, and Amy drifted close to Jo. She reached out to play with Jo's apron string.

"Jo, Marmee told us something that I'm sure was meant for me. You always stand up for me and fight for me. And I'm not nearly good enough. I'm simply a wretched, deplorable creature," Amy finished, enjoying the colorful words despite her distress.

"Oh, oh," Jo sighed in a burst of remorse. "I can't bear this!" She slipped an arm around Amy. "If anyone is wretched, it is myself, so don't give it a thought. Look, here's Meg with the muffins!"

No one has better sisters, Jo thought as she took her place at the table. And no one deserves them less! I must get to Boston today!

After the breakfast things were cleared and washed, the house emptied quickly. Meg went to shop for new ribbons, and Amy tagged along. Beth slipped through the hedge to play the piano for Mr. Laurence.

Jo was able to bundle herself up in her traveling

coat and best bonnet without having to answer any questions.

She wore her stoutest boots and struck out for the Boston road. But once she reached the crossroads, she suddenly felt too shy to hail a stranger. There weren't many homely carts rumbling to market, for it was too late in the morning. And Jo would never hail an elegant carriage. They most likely wouldn't stop for her, anyway.

If only she owned a horse! She could have dressed in her sensible riding habit, hopped onto a fast steed, and galloped her way to Boston. It was just another in a long string of examples of why it could be so inconvenient to be born a girl.

"Will I have to walk the twenty miles?" Jo wondered grimly. "Well, if I must, I must."

She started off down the muddy road. As she tramped, Jo calculated time and distance.

"It will take me at least five hours or more," she muttered. "And that leaves me barely enough time to get to the publisher and return for dinner. I'll be dreadfully late and, worse than that, it will be quite dark. And what if I can't get a ride back to Concord from Boston? I mightn't be home until midnight!"

Jo stopped again and faced the road. She straightened her shoulders and lifted her chin.

"You said you wanted an adventure, Jo March," she told herself. "Well, this is it!"

She heard the clatter of hooves, and an elegant carriage swung around the bend. Jo barely registered the fine, high-stepping horses before quickly turning and pretending to inspect her glove. The carriage was way too grand to hail. And what if Meg heard that Miss Josephine March was seen on the Boston road, attempting to beg a ride?

But to Jo's horror, the carriage drew up. A door creaked. She kept her eyes on her glove.

"Jo, what are you doing out here?" Laurie's voice bellowed.

She turned. Laurie was opening the door and stepping out, not caring how the mud spattered his polished boots.

Oh, bother! If there was one person Jo didn't want to know about her journey, it was Laurie. He would tease and plague her forever!

Jo assumed a dignified air. "I'm going for a walk."

"On this road?" Laurie asked doubtfully. "You'll get spattered with mud, if you don't get run over." He gave her a squinty-eyed, questioning look. "You're fibbing."

"I'm not," Jo said stoutly, "I happen to be fond of this walk—"

"No one walks on this road for pleasure. It's far too dirty," Laurie said decidedly. "Now, you must tell me what you're up to."

"Go away, Teddy," Jo said. Her gray eyes gleamed at him in an alarming way.

"Hanged if I will," Laurie answered promptly. He was not afraid of Jo's mood.

Jo stamped her foot with irritation. "All right, then. I'm going to Boston," she admitted.

"*Walking?*"

"Well, I'd hoped to get a ride."

Laurie let out a whoop. "Wait until Margaret hears about this!"

Jo took a step forward. "Meg mustn't know about it! It's a secret, so keep it, will you Teddy?" she asked in a rush.

Laurie sobered as he saw Jo's serious eyes. "Of course I shall keep it. And you're in luck. I'm on my way to Boston to do an errand for Grandfather."

"Oh, joy!" Jo exclaimed, picking up her skirts. "You can take me along."

"Gladly, old chap." He opened the carriage door, then hesitated. "But I must charge a fare."

"Oh, Teddy, don't plague me today, I couldn't bear it," Jo said crossly.

"I'm afraid I must, Jo," Laurie said. "I'll only give

you a ride to Boston if you tell me your secret. Why must you go?" He ducked his head so that he could look into her stormy face underneath the bonnet. His merry black eyes danced. "So there you have it, my dear. Are you willing to pay the price?"

"Oh, all right, for I must get there," Jo said impatiently. "But you mustn't laugh, or tease, or tell me what an old crosspatch or a wretch I am."

"I promise," Laurie said, holding a hand to his heart.

"You *are* a crosspatch," Laurie said a few minutes later. Jo had recounted her suspicions as they jounced along in the carriage. "And a wretch, and a remarkable goose in the bargain."

"You promised," Jo said, giving him a nudge with her shoulder.

He laughed. "I can't help it, Jo. It isn't like you to be suspicious of your sisters."

"I know," she said with a sigh.

"Of course, you are good at imagining plots, but you usually set them to paper," Laurie said.

"Setting this one to paper was my downfall." She looked out the window at the wintry landscape. "Why are we going so slowly?"

"The roads are bad from all the snow, and then

the thaw," Laurie said, as the carriage struggled out of a deep rut. "Don't fret, Boggs is a good driver. We'll get there."

"Oh, Teddy, I can't bear to hurt their feelings," Jo said with a sigh. "You can't imagine how sweet they were to me this morning. I don't deserve my sisters, I truly don't."

"You do, for you are just as good to them," Laurie said kindly. "You can't remember that at the moment, so I'll have to remind you. Now, we'll be in Boston just past midday, and then after you take back your story I'll buy you a pot of chocolate in a fashionable café I know."

Jo's bleak face brightened. "Nowhere fashionable, please," she said, "but somewhere fascinating, where mysterious people go."

Just then the carriage gave a sudden lurch and then stopped. Laurie stuck his head out of the window.

"What is it, Boggs?"

"It's the wheel, sir," the driver called. "Sorry, sir—it looks like it needs repair."

Jo exchanged worried glances with Laurie. They would never make it to Boston in time!

CHAPTER TWELVE

The Hazards of Pride

*L*aurie and Jo stood by the side of the road, watching Boggs examine the wheel. The news was not good. The damage was worse than Boggs thought. They would need a whole new wheel.

Jo bit her lip. She hated to cry, but she could feel tears gather in her eyes as her throat tightened and threatened to explode into sobs. She imagined how Laurie would react to such a thing. He had never seen her truly cry, and most likely it would frighten him to death. Jo pictured him kneeling in front of her in the mud, anxiously pressing his hand-kerchief on her, and let out a choked sound that was half laugh, half sob.

Laurie looked at her in alarm. Jo grinned to let him know that she wasn't going to dissolve into tears.

He patted her gloved hand. "Jo, I said I would convey you to Boston, and I jolly well shall."

A cart lumbered toward them. In it sat a disagreeable-looking farmer. He wore a hat so re-markably shapeless that Jo imagined it must have been sat on, boiled, then dropped from a tremen-dous height and run over by a mule.

"Excuse me, sir!" Calling out in a loud, cheerful voice, Laurie strode into the middle of the road, holding up a hand.

The cart slowed a bit, but the farmer didn't stop. Laurie had to maintain a steady jog to keep pace with him.

"Would you take pity on a fellow and a young lady and convey us to Boston, sir? We have lost a wheel."

"I've no room, as you see," the farmer said gruffly.

It was true. The back of the cart appeared to be full, with a brown tarp pulled over the items.

And the front seat was crowded with the farmer and several baskets.

"Any place we could squeeze in, you know," Laurie insisted. "I'll pay."

"Whoa! Whoa!" Suddenly the farmer pulled his horse up. "I suppose I could clear a seat or two."

Laurie smiled triumphantly at Jo. "I told you I'd get you there in style!" he called.

"Did you say *in style?*" Jo said with a laugh. She adjusted herself, trying to get comfortable.

Laurie's black eyes gleamed. "I thought you *liked* cabbage," he said.

"I like it on my plate, next to a nice boiled potato," Jo answered. She moved her skirts away from a particularly old specimen. Wrinkling her nose, she added, "And I rather prefer them fresh, don't you?"

Laurie winced as the cart gave a particularly bad jolt. "It's an adventure, Jo."

"I have a feeling that one knows they are having an adventure at the moment they are the most jolly uncomfortable," Jo said, grinning.

Her mood had improved. The brisk air, even the jolting cart, had restored her usual optimism. They would reach Boston in time. Boggs was to meet them at the newspaper office, as soon as possible after he had found his way to the nearest town and repaired the wheel.

They laughed and talked nonsense all the way. The road grew wider and more crowded with vehicles. Soon they were creaking over the cobblestones of the city streets.

Jo peered out of the cart anxiously. "I'm not sure where I am."

"Near the market, I think," Laurie said. He tried to stand, but the cart gave a lurch, and he fell on top of the cabbages. Jo tried not to laugh, but Laurie let out a hearty chuckle at his own clumsiness.

The cart stopped with a jolt. The farmer turned around. "I'm leaving you here."

"Oh, dear," Jo said. Suddenly the streets looked so crowded and strange.

"It's all right, Jo," Laurie said. He stood on tiptoe and peered through the buildings. "Fanueil Hall is just around the corner. We can catch an omnibus to your newspaper office," he assured her.

He jumped off the cart and swung her down. Jo's heels hit the cobblestones. She adjusted her bonnet and hoped she didn't smell of cabbage.

Laurie paid the farmer and they headed down the busy streets. Despite her nervousness, Jo was excited to be in the city. She loved the noise and the crowds and the different faces. Someday, she vowed, she would live in a big city.

They boarded the omnibus and jounced through the streets. It was a surprisingly quick trip to the office of the *Patriot Gazette*.

Jo stood outside the building. It appeared so grimy and forbidding, somehow. Nervousness rattled inside her as she looked at Laurie.

"It's now or never, Teddy," she said.

"Don't fret. No one is better at being charming than you, Jo, when you put your mind to it," Laurie said firmly. "You're my girl, and you'll do fine. I'll be waiting right here for you."

With a last look at the confidence on Laurie's face, Jo pushed open the door.

"No," Mr. Pillson said.

Jo twisted her gloves in her hands. "No?" she repeated.

"No," he said. He picked up the letter he'd been reading. She had been dismissed.

Jo stared at the top of his bald head in dismay. There was no apology, no softness in his manner. He didn't leave much room for argument.

"But Mr. Pillson, it is vital that the story be

withdrawn from publication," Jo tried again. "Not for my welfare, but for . . . other people's. I'll write you a better story—"

Mr. Pillson's watery eyes seemed surprised to still find Jo in his office. He looked at her over his spectacles. "Young lady. The story has been typeset and is at the printer's."

"I could go there," Jo said impulsively. "You wouldn't have to send anyone—"

"The issue has been laid out," Mr. Pillson went on in a weary tone. "And I won't go to the expense and trouble of changing it for the sake of a girlish whim."

Jo drew herself up to her full height. "Girlish whim? I assure you, sir, that not only am I not girlish, I don't have whims, either! And furthermore, if you don't obey my wishes, I shall not send one more story to your periodical!"

Mr. Pillson lifted a corner of his mouth in an almost-smile. "I see. Well. Dear me."

Jo felt herself patronized. Nothing could inflame her more, under ordinary circumstances. But Marmee would tell her to take a deep breath before speaking again, so she did.

The pause allowed her to take another look at the gruff editor. Now Jo saw that his tiny smile wasn't mean, just amused. That encouraged her. Jo tamed her temper and started over.

She clasped her gloved hands together. "Sir, have you ever feared, deep in your heart, that you were about to tragically disappoint those nearest and dearest to you?"

Taken aback, Mr. Pillson was too surprised to do anything but tell the truth. "I suppose," he admitted.

Jo's eyes shone. "Then you'll help me?" she asked eagerly.

The half smile vanished. Mr. Pillson's face once again looked as though it had been carved from marble. He dropped his eyes and concentrated on his letter again. "No. Good day, Miss March."

It was well after dark when Jo and Laurie rolled into Concord at last. Jo climbed down wearily from the carriage.

"Do you want me to come with you, Jo?" Laurie asked sympathetically. "I can explain about the wheel—"

"No, Teddy," Jo said, resigned. "I went to Boston without permission. It was a frightful thing to do, and I've got to face it like a man."

"Perhaps Pillson will reconsider," Laurie said.

His gentle tone told Jo, better than words, that things were hopeless.

She patted him on the arm. "You were such a help, Laurie. At least I know I did my best, thanks to you."

They bid each other good night. Jo headed up the path to the house. She opened the door to the sound of Beth's violin. It stopped when she shut the door, and her sisters rushed into the hall.

"Jo, where were you?" Amy burst out.

"We were worried," Beth said. "You were gone all day, and you almost missed supper!"

"We're having roast chicken," Amy told her.

"You should have told us where you were going," Meg scolded, helping her off with her coat.

"Where did you go, Jo?" Amy asked.

Marmee appeared in the doorway. "Yes, Jo," she said gravely. "Where did you go?"

Jo swallowed. "I went to Boston."

Everyone gasped.

"Without telling us?" Meg asked.

"How did you get there?" Beth asked worriedly.

"I hope you didn't wear those gloves," said Amy. "You should have borrowed Meg's, they're ever so much nicer."

"I went in Laurie's carriage, most of the way," Jo said. "And amid some cabbages, too."

"Cabbages?" Meg asked, wrinkling her nose.

"You went in a farmer's cart?" Marmee asked, concerned.

Suddenly, Jo could not bear their sweet concern another moment. They were all peering at her so worriedly, with such love on their faces. It was agonizing to think that she did not deserve one drop of their concern.

Oh, how I depend on the kindness of my family, she cried silently. And how hard it is to bear when one is bad!

"I was so wrong!" she blurted to Marmee. "And I've never been so sorry about anything in my life."

"About going to Boston?" Marmee asked, puzzled.

"Yes," Jo said. "I mean, no. I mean, oh, everything. . . . What I mean is, my behavior has been unforgivable. I should have left a note. I should have been a better person. It was an impulsive lark, and I don't deserve any supper, so I'm going straight upstairs!" she finished in a rush, her eyes full of unshed tears as she ran up the stairs.

Amy brought her up a plate of chicken, bread, and apples. Beth tapped lightly at her door to give her a tender kiss and her favorite doll for company. Without even scolding her, Meg came in and warmed Jo's hands with her own, then filled a hot water bottle for her cold feet.

The house settled down early that evening as bitter cold set in. Marmee entered Jo's room with her candle and sat on the edge of her bed.

"I'm so sorry for worrying you, Marmee," Jo whispered. "It seems it's all I'm good for, these days."

"Not so," Marmee said with a smile. She picked up Jo's brush and motioned for her to turn.

Grateful, Jo let Marmee brush her long chestnut hair. The smooth, even strokes seemed to ease her troubled mind.

"I can see that you're troubled, dear," Marmee said after a bit. "Would you like to share it?"

"Not yet, please."

Marmee continued to brush. When she was done, she silently braided Jo's hair for the night.

Jo snuggled under the blankets while Marmee turned down the flame of the lantern. She kissed Jo softly on the cheek.

In the dim light, Jo could just make out her mother's gentle face.

"Pray tonight for guidance, dear Jo," Marmee told her. "And trust in yourself and your good heart to find your way."

CHAPTER THIRTEEN

The Celebrated Authoress

"*M*ail from the P.O.!" Beth called a few days later. "Here's a rose for Marmee, and a letter for you, Jo," Beth said, handing the envelope to Jo.

Jo lifted her head from her knitting and took the letter. It was from Laurie, of course. Jo opened it with apprehension. Laurie had said he'd be "on the watch" for the issue of the *Patriot Gazette.*

Over the past few days, Jo had tried to work herself up to break the news that she had cast her sisters as villains in a story that all Concord would read. Time and again she opened her mouth to begin, only to close it again.

She knew she was being a coward. But she wanted a few more days of the sweet home peace before the storm broke. How could she tell those she loved the most that she'd betrayed them? How could she find the words?

Jo scanned the note.

What ho, Jo!

Do not despair! All is not lost, dear chap. Meet me in the garden before tea.

Jo hurried for her coat and scarf. She tramped out through the snow to the garden, where Laurie was waiting. His face was puckered in that way that told her he had a secret he was bursting to tell.

"Your fears are over, Jo," he said. His black eyes danced, and his hair tumbled onto his forehead. He had forgotten his hat. "Look!"

A bulging knapsack sat on the snow. Laurie reached down and opened it with a flourish. After a puzzled glance at him, Jo peeked inside. It was stuffed full of newspapers. She plucked a paper from the top of the pile.

"It's the *Patriot Gazette*," she said. "Oh, dear, it's out at last. Did you check for my story? Is it in?"

Laurie nodded. "It's there, and it's capital, by the

way. But Jo, this isn't just a *few* copies of the paper. It's *every* copy! I bought them all up! Now Meg, Beth, and Amy will never know about it. Nor anybody else in Concord, except for the two of us."

Laurie looked so proud that Jo didn't know whether to laugh or cry.

"Oh, Teddy," she said, with a half sigh, half smile. "You are a dear to try and rescue me. Though I think it's frightful that you spent your money in such fashion," she said, ending with a scold. She looked at the knapsack doubtfully. "Can you take them back?"

"I think not. And why would you want me to?"

"Because you wasted your money, that's why," Jo said. "Which shouldn't surprise me, because you often do."

Laurie looked hurt, and Jo relented.

"It was a kind gesture, and I'll never forget it," she said. "But Teddy, it's no use. I did wrong, and I have to own up to it."

Laurie sighed. "It's a deuce of a problem for a fellow, having a conscience, isn't it?" he said, his black eyes mournful.

"Yes, dear," Jo said. "It is."

*   *   *

Marmee was settled in her corner with her knitting when Jo returned. Amy was sketching, Beth was daydreaming, and Meg was repairing some torn lace.

Jo cleared her throat, and they all looked up.

"I have something for you all to read—" she began, but Amy interrupted her.

"Is it a story of yours, Jo?" she asked excitedly, jumping up.

Beth clapped her hands. "The story you worked so hard on—"

"And it's been published!" Meg exclaimed. "How thrilling!"

Jo twisted the paper in her hands. This was not the way she wanted to begin!

"Don't destroy the paper before we have a chance to read it," Meg said, laughing.

"I need to explain something first," Jo said, in such a sober voice that her sisters quieted. "And when I do, you'll understand why I've been in such a state."

Four concerned faces looked at her. Marmee gave Jo a small nod of encouragement as her knitting dropped to her lap.

"Do you recall that day when I asked for one tiny but thrilling adventure?" Jo asked with a grimace. "Well, I suppose I got my wish, but not quite the way I imagined. You see, I let myself fall into the blackest of moods and did something little and mean. My own guilt twisted my mind. Because *I* had betrayed, I thought even those I loved most were capable of betrayal. And I'm so dreadfully sorry," Jo finished in a whisper.

"I don't understand, Jo," Meg said.

"You will," Jo said. She handed her the *Patriot Gazette*. "Meg, will you read this aloud?" she asked.

CHAPTER FOURTEEN

Plain and Good

*M*eg cleared her throat and began. Marmee picked up her knitting again. Amy curled up on the sofa next to Beth.

Jo couldn't bear to watch their faces. Instead, she stared into the fire so hard that her eyes began to tear.

Meg used her dramatic talents to bring the story to life. She acted out all the parts and read the suspenseful events in a colorful, thrilling voice.

At last, she came to the end. Meg's voice dropped to a low, portentous tone as she read the last words.

"As she gazed upon the white, still faces of her two dead sisters and thought of the one banished far away, Dove could not forestall a solitary tear. Once, she had longed to cherish these faces, to see them across hearth and table down through the long years. After all the plots and devices they had used, the terrors they had employed, how strange that she could love them still!"

Meg's voice died away. A collective sigh echoed through the room.

Jo couldn't turn. She knew if she tried to speak, she would croak like a frog. She waited for stormy tears and accusations to rain upon her.

Meg sighed. "I'm glad Miranda died in the end," she said decidedly. "She was a horrid creature."

"I love the name Amaryllis," Amy said dreamily. "It's a pity she was so bad."

"I'm glad Beatrice didn't die, and got to tend geese in the end," Beth remarked thoughtfully. "It really wasn't her fault that sweet Dove got locked in the garret, you know. She was weak, perhaps, but not evil."

Jo couldn't believe her ears. She rose and paced in front of them.

"But don't you see?" she burst out. "*You* are those sisters! I was angry with all of you, and I turned you into them. Amaryllis has golden curls and is fond of sketching. Miranda is the oldest, and Beatrice is shy with strangers—" Jo felt as though she were choking, and couldn't go on.

"We know you based them on us," Meg said calmly. "It's only a story, Jo. You make up the most appalling things to amuse us all the time."

"At least you gave Amaryllis an aristocratic nose," Amy said. "That was kind of you, Jo. You're the best sister!"

Jo's knees felt weak, and she sank down on the carpet. She looked up at her sisters in astonishment. "You mean, you don't despise me? And what if others read the story?"

Beth smiled. "I doubt they would recognize the March girls in such evil creatures."

"I wouldn't mind," Amy said. "It would be quite thrilling, I think."

"I think I could mind, but I don't believe there's any danger of it," Meg decided.

Jo bit her lip. "So you don't mind that I made you all act so horridly to poor Dove?"

"Not at all," Meg declared. "Who will know, except for us, and Laurie? We'll all have a good laugh about being so wicked. I think you should turn this into a play, and we'll put on one of our theatricals."

"It would be terribly and desperately romantic to die clutching pearls," Amy said. She threw herself back on the sofa in a dramatic gesture, clutching at an imaginary necklace.

"And it's only make-believe," Beth added. "It's like playing with dolls."

Meg frowned. "But I still don't understand what you meant about being beastly to us."

Jo bowed her head. She knotted her hands together in her lap. "It's time for me to ' 'fess up.' First, I thought you all had planned that terrible day, just to teach me a lesson—"

"Why ever would we do such a thing!" Meg gasped.

"Oh, Jo," Beth said softly.

"I know you wouldn't," Jo said. "I was just so tired and worn out, I didn't know what to think. And I had heard you laughing behind the door—"

"But it was so funny, Jo!" Meg said with a giggle.

"Don't you agree?" she asked, looking at her sister anxiously.

"It was a comedy fit for the stage," Jo said with a grin. "But I suppose my dignity suffered a bit. And then when you arranged that glorious tea party, I was afraid that you'd read my manuscript and were afraid I'd publish it, so you were being nice to me so I'd change it—"

"Jo!" Beth exclaimed.

"But you all kept quoting from it!" Jo insisted. "Or, at least, I thought you did. Meg called me a wounded dove one day—"

"Well, you were acting like one," Meg pointed out primly.

"And Amy said she would die happy if she had a strand of pearls," Jo continued.

"That's because she saw the pearls Aunt March was saving for the first one of us to marry," Meg said with an exasperated but affectionate look at Amy. "Amy, you shouldn't say such things."

"And you shouldn't be so interested in pearl necklaces," Marmee chided with a frown.

"I'm not, *really*," Amy said. "Well, at least I try not to be."

Jo slipped her hand into Beth's. "Even dear,

sweet Beth said that she felt sorry for the poor geese, just like Beatrice would."

Amy giggled. "But Jo, you were the one to speak of sparing the geese, when you rewrote *A Christmas Carol*, remember?"

"Well, bless my boots, I believe I did," Jo recalled with a laugh.

"Besides, Beth feels sorry for the geese every Christmas," Meg said, giving Beth an affectionate smile. She turned to Jo. "Don't you see, Jo, that you gave your villains just a pinch of each of us, enough to make them human? And that human quality is precisely the thing that made the story feel so true."

"You are all so good!" Jo cried. "I don't know how I could have suspected you of trickery. I'm ashamed of myself." She gazed down at her twisted hands in her lap. "It's unforgivable."

It was Marmee's soft voice that made her lift her head. "Nothing is unforgivable, Jo."

When Jo looked up, her sisters were smiling at her. What could she do but smile in return?

"Well, I'm sure I don't deserve such forgiveness, but I suppose I'll have to accept it," she said ruefully.

"I'm afraid we must insist," Meg told her in the prim voice she used when correcting her sisters.

Everyone laughed heartily, Jo hardest of all.

Growing thoughtful, Jo leaned back against the sofa and stared into the fire. "I learned my lesson, hard though it was. The terrible thing about that whisper of distrust is that it has a tendency to spread to the most innocent places in your heart. So I've learned that you can't let distrust in at all, not a lick of it. You must swing the gate against it and lock it out of your heart at once."

"That's a good lesson, Jo," Marmee said. "For all of us."

Jo rose and went to kneel at her mother's chair. "Marmee, I know this fee is more than I've ever received," she said. "And I know the household needs it dreadfully. I was planning to buy new things for you all with it. But instead I'd like to give you the money for the Christmas baskets for the soldiers and the poor. Some good should come out of my foolishness, don't you think? I'm glad that you all like the story. But somehow, I'll never be very proud of it myself."

Marmee reached out to caress Jo's hair. "I think that's a fine idea," she said softly. "Do you see now that if you write out of bitterness and the desire to hurt, you'll never be happy with your work or yourself? Your gift is a powerful one, Jo. You must use it wisely, and with love."

Jo nodded. She looked around at the cozy room. The fire blazed cheerfully, and the light played on the faces of her sisters. Soon it would be time for supper. The night would grow darker, and colder, but she would be warm and safe, surrounded by a circle of love.

At that moment, Jo knew that there was nowhere she'd rather be in the wide, wide world than right where she was. She would always long for adventure. But she would always treasure her home.

"Miranda, Beatrice, and Amaryllis were rather desperately romantic," Jo said. "But I have to confess that I prefer my plain and good Meg, Beth, and Amy."

"As we prefer our troublesome Jo," Meg finished affectionately.